KU-623-117

This Walker book belongs to:

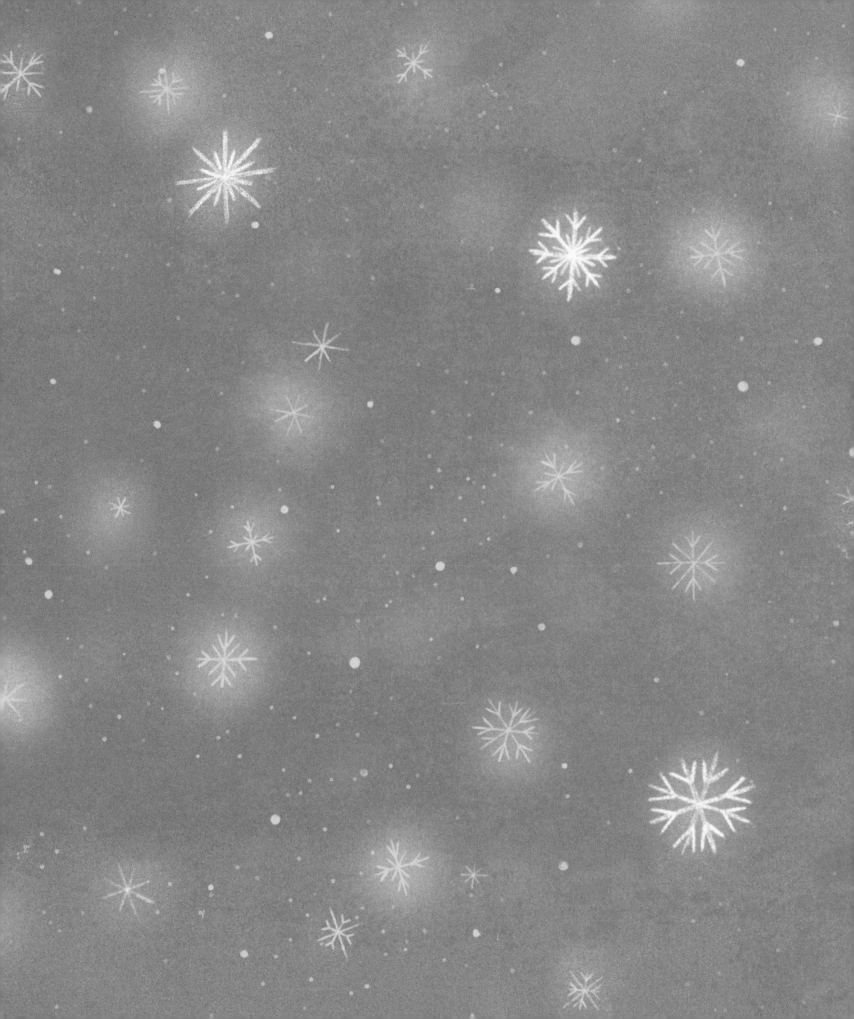

To Justin, Kim, Ruth, and Will, who make Christmases merry and magical ~ *P.T.*

For Jenna ~ *J.*

First published 2017 by Walker Books Ltd, 87 Vauxhall Walk, London SE11 5HJ · This edition published 2018 · Text © 2017 Patricia Toht · Illustrations © 2017 Jarvis · The right of Patricia Toht and Jarvis to be identified as author and illustrator respectively of this work has been asserted by them in accordance with the Copyright, Designs and Patents Act 1988 · This book has been typeset in OPTIMemphis · Printed in Italy · All rights reserved. No part of this book may be reproduced, transmitted or stored in an information retrieval system in any form or by any means, graphic, electronic or mechanical, including photocopying, taping and recording, without prior written permission from the publisher. · British Library Cataloguing in Publication Data: a catalogue record for this book is available from the British Library · ISBN 978-1-4063-7977-8 · www.walker.co.uk · 10 9 8 7 6 5 4 3 2

Pick a PINE TREE

Patricia Toht   illustrated by Jarvis

WALKER BOOKS
AND SUBSIDIARIES
LONDON · BOSTON · SYDNEY · AUCKLAND

Pick a pine tree
from the lot —

PINE
TREES
FOR
SALE

slim and tall
or short and squat.
One with spiky needle clumps,
scaly bark, or sappy bumps.

Long, straight limbs
or branches bent —
mmm! Just smell
that piney scent!

DECORATIONS

Lift the tree
above your head,
bundle it upon your sled,

or, if you live very far,
bring it home
atop your car.

Now...

Move aside a lamp or chair —
clear away a section where
your tree will sit, tall and grand,
snug and sturdy, in its stand.

Trim the trunk
a little bit,
just enough
so it will fit.

Slip it in and
turn screws tight —
they will hold
your tree upright.

Fill with water
to the brink.
Give your thirsty
tree a drink!
Then...

Find the trimmings
stored within
bulging boxes, rusty tins,
paper bags, a wooden case.

Bring them to that
special place,
there, beside your tree.
But wait...

Don't decorate alone!
Call some people
on the phone.

Ask your friends
to come and stay —

host a
decorating
day!

SANTA
STOP HERE

Stretch along some
fairy lights,
a coloured mix
or simply white.
Fat, round bulbs
or pointy tips,
bubble lights or
candle clips.

Start up top
or near the base,
wrap around
and tuck in place.
Next...

Hang ornaments
upon your tree.
What kind of trinkets
will they be?

Jolly Santas.
Dancing elves.
Wooden reindeer.
Jingle bells.
Lacy snowflakes.
Paper dolls.

Candy canes and
bright glass balls.
With loops of thread
or wire hooks,
hang them all in
little nooks.

MERRY CHRISTMAS

Add the final
touches now —
garlands strung
from bough to bough.

Strands of tinsel
on the tips,
falling down
in silver drips.
    Then...

Grab a footstool.
Climb right up.
Set something
wonderful on top.

A golden star.
A velvet bow.
An angel dressed
in flowing robes.

Lay a tree skirt
down below.
Add some houses
flecked with snow,

FOR
YOU

a train that chugs
around a track,
secret presents
in a sack.

At last, it's time
to make it SHINE!
Plug in lights
along the floor.

LOOK!
It's not a pine tree anymore.

It's a ...

CHRISTMAS TREE!

Gather round the tree to sing, let your joyful voices ring.

Celebrate as night-time falls...

Merry CHRISTMAS, one and all!

Praise for *Pick a Pine Tree*:

"A sprightly, unashamedly Christmassy book" *Observer*

"If you haven't put up your tree yet, this will have you
racing to the attic for the fairy lights" *Daily Mail*

"If you're going to pick a Christmas book, you'll struggle
to find one more festively atmospheric" *The Herald*

"Pick this delightful story for a Christmas storytime, for library
collections, or for family reading around the Christmas tree"
Kirkus, Starred Review

"All the magic of Christmas is gathered in these words and pictures"
Julia Eccleshare's Book of the Month, LoveReading

"The evocative book ends with a sparkling switch on of the lights
that will make every heart soar" *Junior Magazine*

"Toht's rhyming text is greatly illuminated by Jarvis's illustrations,
which imbue each step with holiday warmth"
The Horn Book

Look out for
Pick a Pumpkin